HILDA BOSWELL'S
RED
TREASURY

Stories • Poems • Rhymes

CARNIVAL

Hansel and Gretel

On the edge of a forest lived a woodcutter with his two children. Their names were Hansel and Gretel. For a long time the children were very happy. They would go off with their father in the early morning and stay near him while he worked. They kept themselves busy gathering berries and nuts and mushrooms, and Gretel would pick bunches of wild flowers.

But everything changed when their father married again, for their stepmother turned out to be a cruel woman who hated the children.

"There are too many mouths to feed," she complained to her husband. "What a quantity of food these children eat, and us so poor! I tell you, we must get rid of them."

This made the woodcutter very uneasy.

Nevertheless, the stepmother nagged him until one night, when Hansel lay awake in bed, he heard his father agree to take the children into the forest and leave them there.

Next morning, before the grown-ups were awake, Hansel crept outside and filled his pockets with pebbles. When they had had some breakfast, their father took them into the forest, farther than ever before. "Wait for me here," he said.

He lit a fire of brushwood to keep them warm and then sadly turned his back on them.

When it grew dark, Hansel said; "Father will not come back, but I have left a trail of pebbles and we can find our own way."

As soon as the moon came up, the little white pebbles shone like stars and led them all the way home to their father's cottage.

No one could have been more surprised than the stepmother.

That night, Hansel heard her say to their father: "I will not have it! You must take them deeper into the forest this time."

Sadly over-ruled by his wife, the woodcutter took his children even farther into the forest. Unhappily, Hansel had not been able to gather pebbles, for the stepmother had taken care to lock the cottage door. "Do not worry," whispered Hansel to Gretel. "I have crumbled the bread I got for breakfast and have dropped it on the way."

But there was no trail, for the birds had flown down and eaten every crumb. Gretel began to cry, but Hansel said: "Look! There is smoke rising above the trees. It may be a woodman's hut."

The children hurried through the trees and soon found themselves in a little clearing. There stood the strangest little house they had ever seen. Its walls were made of gingerbread and its roof was made of cake, and all the windows were made of barley sugar.

Soon they were nibbling away at the little house for they were very hungry. Hansel broke off a piece of the roof and Gretel broke off a piece of the window.

Then out popped a little old woman. "Come in, my dears!" she said in the friendliest voice.

The old woman made a delicious meal for them, and when they had eaten their fill, she led them upstairs where there were two little beds. What a kind old woman she seemed to be! But, dear me! she was really a most wicked witch.

Next morning when Gretel woke up, Hansel was gone. "Where is my brother?" she asked the old woman, but all the reply she got was:

"Fetch some firewood! The oven must be kept hot."

When she was fetching the wood, Gretel found Hansel locked in the chicken-house.

"You must find a way to save me," cried Hansel, "for she plans to cook and eat me!"

And this was exactly what she meant to do, and she had chosen Hansel because he was bigger and plumper.

All day long Gretel carried in wood and the witch piled it on to the fire until the little kitchen was as hot as hot could be.

Every time she passed the chicken-house Gretel would whisper to Hansel; "Do not worry, Hansel, I will think of a way to save you!"

"Surely the oven must be hot enough now," said the witch impatiently. "Put your head in and tell me if it is hot enough," she said to Gretel.

"Not yet," said Gretel.

The witch put on more wood and told Gretel to test it again. "Is it hot enough now?" she asked.

"Not yet," said Gretel.

"Silly goose!" said the witch. "It *must* be hot enough! I will test it myself."

And she put her head in the oven.

Quick as lightning, Gretel gave the witch a push that sent her headlong into the oven. Gretel slammed the door and fixed the bolt. Then she ran out to Hansel.

Gretel broke the lock on the chicken-house door and she and Hansel ran back to the cottage. "What will you give me if I let you out?" said Hansel to the witch in the oven.

"I will give you my magic stick," said the witch. "It will obey your command and turn anything it touches into nice things to eat. Take it! I don't care! Only *please* let me out!"

"And do you promise to be good from now on and eat no more poor children?" asked Hansel.

"Yes, yes, I promise!" wailed the witch.

Hansel snatched up the stick and Gretel unlatched the oven door, and out stepped the old woman, rather hot and bothered but smiling. From that day on she was a good, kind, old woman and loved the children dearly.

She cared for Hansel and Gretel like a loving grandmother and they lived with her in the magic cottage.

Hansel only had to say to the magic stick: "Bring my father here!" and they would hear the woodcutter knocking on the chocolate door of the gingerbread cottage and his kind voice saying: "How are you, my dears?"

GRIMM

I Wish I Lived in a Caravan

I wish I lived
   in a caravan,
With a horse to drive,
   like a pedlar man!
Where he comes from nobody knows,
   Or where he goes to, but on he goes.
His caravan has windows too,
   And a chimney of tin that the smoke comes through.
He has a wife, with a baby brown,
   And they go riding from town to town.

MY SHADOW

I have a little shadow that goes in and
                     out with me,
And what can be the use of him is more
                     than I can see.
He is very, very like me from the heels
                     up to the head;
And I see him jump before me, when I jump
                     into my bed.

The funniest thing about him is the way
                he likes to grow—
Not at all like proper children, which
                is always very slow;
For he sometimes shoots up taller like an india-rubber ball,
And he sometimes gets so little that
                there's none of him at all.

He hasn't got a notion of how children
                ought to play.
And can only make a fool of me in every
                sort of way.
He stays so close beside me, he's a
                coward, you can see;
I'd think shame to stick to nursie as
                that shadow sticks to me!

One morning, very early, before the sun
was up,
I rose and found the shining dew on every
buttercup;
But my lazy little shadow, like an arrant
sleepy-head;
Had stayed at home behind me and was
fast asleep in bed.

ROBERT LOUIS STEVENSON

Snow White and the Seven Dwarfs

Once upon a time, in a faraway land, there
lived a lovely Princess called Snow White.
She had a skin as white as snow, hair as black as
ebony, and lips as red as cherries.

Her mother had died when she was very
little, and some time afterwards her father
married again and brought a new Queen to the
palace.

The new Queen was very beautiful, but she
was so proud and haughty that she could not
bear anyone to be prettier than herself. She had
a wonderful magic mirror, and when she
stepped before it and said:

"Mirror, mirror on the wall,
who is the fairest of us all?"

The mirror would reply:

"You are the fairest, Lady Queen."

But the Queen could not help but notice that little Snow White was growing prettier with every day that passed, and one day, when the Queen spoke to her mirror she did not get the answer she expected. Said the mirror:

"O Queen, your loveliness is rare,
But Snow White seems to all more fair."

The Queen flew into a passion and made up her mind that Snow White must die. So she called one of her huntsmen and ordered him to take the little princess into the huge forest that surrounded the palace and leave her there to die.

The thought of doing such a dreadful thing broke the huntsman's heart but he was too afraid of the Queen to refuse to obey her commands. So he took Snow White a little way into the forest and left her there, hoping she would be found and cared for by some woodcutter's family.

Poor Snow White was alone in the great forest and did not know what to do. So she began to run, and she ran until she was quite tired out.

At last she came to a clearing where a little cottage stood. She knocked timidly on the door and called out: "Is there anyone there?"

There was no answer, and since the door was unlocked, she thought she might go in and rest for a little while.

The cottage was very neat. The table was laid with seven little plates, seven little mugs, seven little knives and forks, and seven little spoons. Seven little chairs stood round the table, and seven little beds stood against the wall. Snow White lay down on one of the beds and fell fast asleep. Soon the owners of the cottage returned. They were seven dwarfs.

They had been digging for ore in the mountains all day long

and they were very tired. They were looking
forward to supper and a warm bed. It was
almost dark, so they lit their seven little candles
and looked about the cottage. At first they
noticed that the chairs had been moved a little
bit, and then they noticed that the plates had
been moved a little bit, and they got very angry
for they were sure that someone had been in
the cottage. They were such neat and tidy little
men that they noticed at once if anything was
out of place. But when they found Snow White
fast asleep on one of their beds, they could not
be angry any more.

They thought she was the prettiest creature they had ever seen. They shook her gently awake and said: "Who are you?"

"I'm called Snow White," she said, and she told them the whole sad story of how her wicked stepmother had the huntsman leave her in the forest to die of hunger, or be killed by the wild animals.

"Shame!" cried one.

"Poor child!" said another.

"You must stay here," said a third.

"We would like that," said a fourth.

"And we'll look after you," said a fifth.

"You could keep house for us," said a sixth.

"And never see the wicked Queen again," said a seventh.

Snow White could have cried from happiness, the little men were so kind to her.

"But remember," they said, "when we are away at work you must never let anyone come into the cottage because if your stepmother should find out you are here she would certainly try to harm you."

Snow White was very happy keeping house for the dwarfs.

One day, an old woman knocked at the door. She looked so weary that Snow White asked her to come in and rest a while, for what harm can an old apple woman do me? She thought.

But what Snow White did not know was that the old apple woman was the wicked Queen in disguise. She had learned from the magic mirror that Snow White was alive and living in the forest in the cottage of the dwarfs.

Full of fury, she puzzled how she might get rid of her stepdaughter and she decided that this time she must do it herself to be sure there would be no mistake. So she filled a basket with apples and into the biggest, rosiest apple she put poison enough to kill ten men. Then she set out.

"What a kind child you are!" said the old woman when she had rested for a few minutes. "You must taste one of my apples. See, here is the rosiest of them all – and it will be the sweetest. Try it, my dear."

To please the old woman, Snow White took the apple and bit into the shiny red skin. The apply did not taste sweet. It tasted very bitter.

The piece of apple was no sooner in Snow White's mouth than she fell senseless to the floor. She turned as pale as death. One look satisfied the wicked Queen that she had nothing more to fear and she left the cottage laughing and chuckling because her plot had succeeded so well.

When the dwarfs came home from the mine in the evening and saw Snow White lying so pale and still they were certain she was dead.

They were heart-broken.

"How can we put anything so lovely into the dark earth?" they said to each other.

So they made a glass coffin and laid it on top of a little hill under some tall trees.

But how dreary life was without Snow White! How they missed her in the cottage when they came home from the mine in the evenings! Time passed, and one day a Prince came riding by.

He gazed at the beautiful girl and could not help falling in love with her. The dwarfs told him her sad story and the Prince asked if he might take her back to his palace.

Since he was so much in love, the dwarfs agreed and helped him to carry the precious burden. But one of the dwarfs stumbled and gave the coffin a little jolt. The piece of poisoned apple fell from Snow White's mouth and she opened her eyes and smiled. The dwarfs were overjoyed, and minded only a little bit as they watched Snow White ride off with the Prince to his own country.

GRIMM

Two Little Kittens

Two little kittens, one stormy night,
  Began to quarrel and then to fight.
One had a mouse and the other had none,
  And that's the way the quarrel began.

The old woman seized her sweeping broom,
  And swept the two kittens right out of the room.

The ground was all covered with frost and snow,
  And the two little kittens had nowhere to go.
So they lay them down on the mat at the door,
  While the old woman finished sweeping the floor.

Then in they crept, as quiet as mice,
  All wet with the snow, and as cold as ice.
For they found it much better, that stormy night,
  To lie down and sleep, than to quarrel and fight.

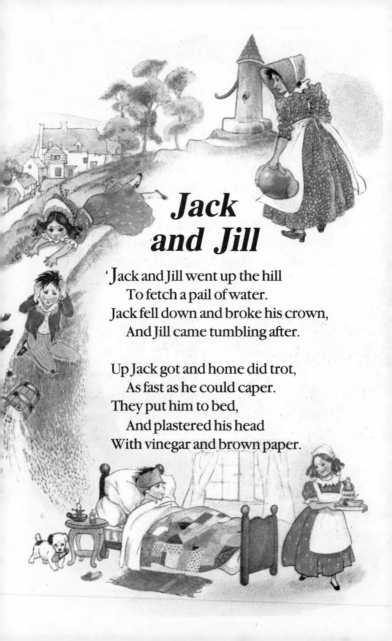

Jack and Jill

'Jack and Jill went up the hill
    To fetch a pail of water.
Jack fell down and broke his crown,
    And Jill came tumbling after.

Up Jack got and home did trot,
    As fast as he could caper.
They put him to bed,
    And plastered his head
With vinegar and brown paper.

BAA BAA BLACK SHEEP

Baa, Baa, black sheep, have you any wool?
Yes, sir, yes, sir, three bags full:
One for my master and one for my dame,
And one for the little boy
that lives
down
the
lane.

Carnival
An imprint of Children's Division
of the Collins Publishing Group
8 Grafton Street, London W1X 3LA

Published by Carnival 1988

ISBN 0 00 194484 3

Printed & bound in Great Britain by
PURNELL BOOK PRODUCTION LIMITED
A MEMBER OF BPCC plc

HOPPER
COT